MAPMAKERS
AND THE
LOST MAGIC

Mapmakers and the Lost Magic was written with pencil and paper before being transferred to a Word document. It was drawn and colored digitally in Photoshop and lettered with the artist's own handwritten font.

Text copyright © 2022 by Cameron Chittock
Cover art and interior illustrations copyright © 2022 by Amanda Castillo

All rights reserved. Published in the United States by RH Graphic, an imprint of Random House Children's Books, a division of Penguin Random House LLC, New York.

RH Graphic with the book design is a trademark of Penguin Random House LLC.

Visit us on the web! RHKidsGraphic.com • @RHKidsGraphic

Educators and librarians, for a variety of teaching tools, visit us at RHTeachersLibrarians.com

Library of Congress Cataloging-in-Publication Data is available upon request.
ISBN 978-0-593-17287-2 (hardcover) — ISBN 978-0-593-17286-5 (paperback)
ISBN 978-0-593-17289-6 (ebook) — ISBN 978-0-593-17288-9 (lib. bdg.)

Designed by Patrick Crotty
Title design by Walter Parenton

MANUFACTURED IN CHINA
10 9 8 7 6 5 4 3 2 1
First Edition

A comic on every bookshelf.

MAPMAKERS
AND THE
LOST MAGIC

Written by

CAMERON CHITTOCK

Illustrated by

AMANDA CASTILLO

For Tay
—C.C.

Para mi abuelo. Te quiero por siempre.
Este es mi adiós para ti.
—A.C.

Random House Graphic Presents

MAPMAKERS
and the Lost Magic

Written by Cameron Chittock
Illustrated by Amanda Castillo

Wrong direction. Not **Alden** . . .

Out **there**. The horizon. Where anything is possible.

It's nothing but **clouds**. Big gray clouds, all year round.

You really want to leave Alden one day, don't you?

Leave behind the same little town I've known my whole life?

Yeah. I really do.

13

15

Hmm.
Your satchel is quite a ragged old thing, isn't it? The patchwork . . .

There's only one place capable of such . . . creative craftsmanship.

"Let's go pay your mother a visit, Miss Rose."

21

They were outside Alden's boundary.

And that was before they made a **scene** in the brick pit.

Terrorizing the people working to keep this town afloat.

That's not true —

Alidade! Not another word.

24

Property of H. Rose

Sorry, Ma.

Ugh.

Lewis can never know about this.

coff coff

Blech!

Alden?

What are **you** doing here?

That doesn't look right . . .

Hey!

49

50

KAFF
KAFF

Are you okay??

Did that **sound** okay?!

What can I do? I've got all kinds of stuff in my satchel . . .

No. I know what happens when people like **you** try to help . . .

People like **me**?

Yes. **People.** You are a person, are you not?

Why . . . why is **my town** on this map? I've never seen any of these places before.

What do you mean you've never —

—what's happened to the Valley, Alidade Rose?

Where are the **Mapmakers**?

I—I—

WHERE ARE THEY?

Wait—!

That . . . that was . . .

Awesome.

55

"...the sooner we're free."

You were right. No surprises—this is the worst.

We're almost done.

Almost done?!

And you just . . . found the doorknob?

When we were running from the Night Coats and got separated, it . . . appeared. Like magic.

This place has all sorts of magic.

And it's like they say in books—the best magic . . .

. . . requires a little . . .

. . . more . . .

. . . work.

... you're a what, now?

You've never heard of the Memris?!

"Mapmakers bring us to life so we might guide humanity to live in harmony with the natural world.

"We are protectors of the land and peace."

Or ... we **used** to be.

But, Mr. Blue, sir, um — if you're proof of all this power, how come you're so tiny?

I think what Lewis means is . . . **something** happened to you. Right?

Yes. If I am this weak, it's because my map no longer reflects the land. It must have . . . **changed.**

I imagine we have the Night Coats to thank for that.

He knows about the Night Coats?

Oh yes, very well.

The way of the Mapmakers is not the fantastic life you're imagining.

It's a life in **ruins**.

The Night Coats are still in power. The Mapmakers **failed**.

Only **people** are capable of creating an end so bleak.

The best thing for you to do is forget this ever happened.

Maybe he's right, Al.

Maybe it's time to head back.

Hm. Okay, Alidade Rose. I will teach you how to be a Mapmaker.

But if you give me one reason to think this is a mistake, that's the end of it.

Now . . . it's time to see what happened to my Valley.

The what?

Our **river**! All that time with my map and you failed to notice the giant blue streak?

Well . . . there's no river here.

Don't think there's ever been one.

Oh, there was. And it . . .

. . . it was **everything.**

No wonder I'm so weak. If the river dried up . . . we have more work to do than I realized.

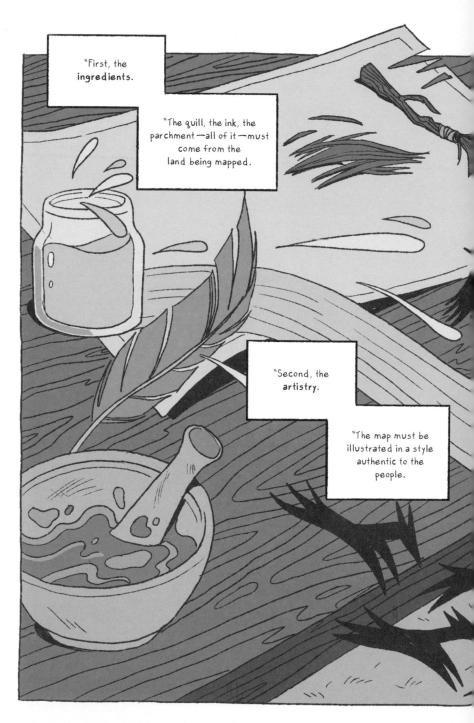

"First, the **ingredients.**

"The quill, the ink, the parchment—all of it—must come from the land being mapped.

"Second, the **artistry.**

"The map must be illustrated in a style authentic to the people.

"And finally, the **accuracy**.

"The map must properly convey its land down to the detail."

If any **one** of the tenets is not precise, the map is useless.

Once completed, a Mapmaker adds their signature to bind it all together: the **compass rose**.

I can teach you, but **you** will have to reintroduce me to the land. I ... do not recognize it.

That's okay, we know it pretty well.

Now, to prove you can be in tune with the world around you, you must find your **first ingredient**.

...a **lightning** **worm** hive!

They're kinda cute. In their own...gross way. What do we do with them?

We smash 'em.

WHAT?!

I spent many summers cleaning up this **awful** patch.

Really?

I know this seems like the end of the world. I used to **rage** against it.

But the bricks are our livelihood.

Before you or I were born . . . Alden was desperate for work. People went hungry. It was a dire time for our town.

The **Night Coats** showed our people how to make the bricks and turn this pit into something useful: a second chance.

It's grueling work, but it's tradition for everyone to chip in.

"...I've got a feeling things are going to start looking up."

It's not so bad.

It's **quilting**, Lewis. It's pretty bad.

Ugh. Why can't I figure this ingredient thing out?

I keep thinking about what Blue said, hoping I'll pick up some clue. But I've got nothing.

I'm sorry, Al. I wish there was some way I could help.

CRRK

SHHK

THUD

CRRK

SHHK

THUD

What—

—is that?

CRRK

Left alone for years and now I can't even get a good night's sleep!

SHHK

THUD

109

But then . . . how would a Mapmaker ever find it? Don't they always know where they're going?

Hah. No. **Clearly**, or maybe the Night Coats would not have **won**!

Mapmakers thrive because they are **comfortable** not knowing where they are going.

Everyone is lost, in a way.

Embracing the challenge—**that** is the key to being a Mapmaker.

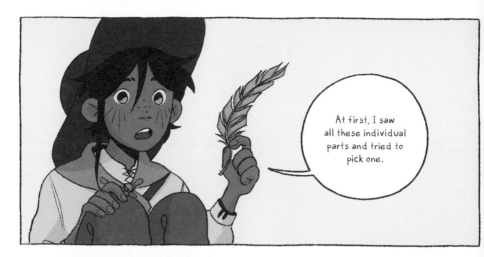

At first, I saw all these individual parts and tried to pick one.

But really, each piece is part of the **whole**.

The tree isn't **broken**, it's a home for the worms.

The worms provide for the ravens.

Who in turn protect the nest.

The feather is the thing I can take with me that will remind me of **each** piece. Without disturbing any of them.

Well done, Alidade Rose.

Thanks, Blue.

"What might seem mundane to the natural eye . . .

". . . can help create wonders."

"But it is done so
we might expand
our horizons . . ."

". . . and help others
do the same."

All right, time for the compass rose. The final piece.

As soon as I finish this compass rose, you're going back to full strength. Are you excited? Nervous?

Impatient.

All alone, Mr. Briar?

I haven't seen you with Miss Rose as much these days.

She prefers it that way.

Ah. I'm sorry to hear that.

I hoped you'd rub off on her. Keep her from chasing the dangers that lie beyond town limits.

Dangers?

You all clean?

Yeah.

Good. Here, help me with the dishes.

What's wrong, hon?

Ma, what'd you and dad love so much about Alden? That makes you so . . . crazy about it?

Heh. Well, Alden is like most things in life —it is what you make of it. And your father and I made it **ours.**

133

What is it?

Strange. I . . . do not know.

I don't remember seeing it on the map. It's like it doesn't exist.

Let's see what we can learn from a closer inspection.

What **was** that, sir? The **thing** she was holding?

A remnant from a time gone by.

Excuse me. E-excuse me.

Alidade!!

ALIDADE!!

ALIDADE!

Hello?

It's those dark bricks.

"Whatever they're made of, they had a magic of their own.

"And they're not on the map."

Whatever they are, they don't belong here. Like the Night Coats.

I just need more time to study them.

"... the Constable is going to have eyes on that area nonstop.

"We'd need the whole town to distract them!"

Okay, Lewis . . .

". . . you can do this."

I can do this.
I can do this.

Hello??

Where is everybody?

Lewis?!

"...whatever Alidade needs."

I ... I thought you said people were **hiding** out?

They are. They're just out **here** now.

167

Mr. Briar, I understand you're upset that your friend is gone, but it's no excuse for childish behavior.

Childish behavior? I saw this more as courageous defiance.

Mr. Briar, when I said you were a man of the people, I had something far less rebellious in mind.

If you do this, there's no going back.

I'm happy with where we're going.

"We"?

Mr. Briar, where is Miss Rose?

kaff kaff

Yeah . . .

. . . this definitely wasn't on our map.

You're making a mistake.

No, we're making a **choice**.

Now it's your turn.

What'll it be?

It's the **river**. Isn't it?

The Night Coats buried it down here for so long, everyone forgot it existed.

But the mosquitoes sensed it somehow.

And Blue . . . **he** remembered.

And **what**—you want to bring back the past? Erase progress for something you don't even **remember**?

You're lucky to grow up as you did! The Night Coats —this **dam** —kept you safe from the dangers the river **invites**!

Is it ready, Al?

Don't call attention to it—heaven forbid she realizes she's **quilting.**

It's not quilting **exactly.**

It counts! I'm counting it.

". . . we'll find it together."

To Be Continued

Autumn Squirrel

SHINY FUR = HEALTHY SQUIRREL

suuuper SOFt!! softer than Blue!

A small rodent with a bushy tail and tufts on their ears. Named for their coat of fur that blends in with fall leaves. Ma thinks there are more of these critters in Alden than people.

Personality: Bold.
Not scared of anything.
Food: Any kind of nuts or seeds they can find. (And if we're not careful, our lunch.)

this CaRDiNAL let Me get close! Blue SAid this FeAtheR WAS its gift to Me!

Black-Bellied Cardinal

A red bird with twin black markings on their face and chest. They can be found all year round, and with their constant singing, you won't miss them.

Personality: Lewis says they're "smug."
Call: A high-pitched and drawn-out *stweee-pree-pree*.

looks like the sunrise

Me → and dad

LEAF

Dawnberry

Round berries that grow on a small shrub and are ready for picking in the middle of summer.

Coloring: Reddish pink.
Like a sunrise.
Taste: They have a sweet, floral taste. Dad would always wait until late summer to pick his so they tasted just a liiittle tart.

Twirl for something cool

smells like A summer breeze

Teal Lily

A wildflower found on the woodland floors. Inner and outer petals are different lengths and colors, but if you twirl them, they show a pretty teal ring. (What we didn't use for the map we gave to Lewis's sister. They're her favorite.)

231

Lewis Briar's Practical Guide to Quilting, Knitting, and Crafts of All Kinds

Quilting is the craft of choice for the Valley. A tradition passed down for years. While I am no expert, these are my tips for becoming a master quilt maker. (You can do it!)

Tip #1: Find a quilting buddy! Crafts are always best when done with others.

Tip #2: Quilting can be dangerous. Before getting started, make sure you have bandages at the ready just in case. (I learned this the hard way. Twice.)

Tip #3: Start small. Squares five-inch by five-inch are great for beginners.

Tip #4: Choose a design that means a lot to you! When you put your heart into it, the final piece will only be better.

Tip #5: Mistakes happen. Sometimes a lot. But that's okay! No one becomes a master quilt maker overnight.

Tip #6: Have fun!

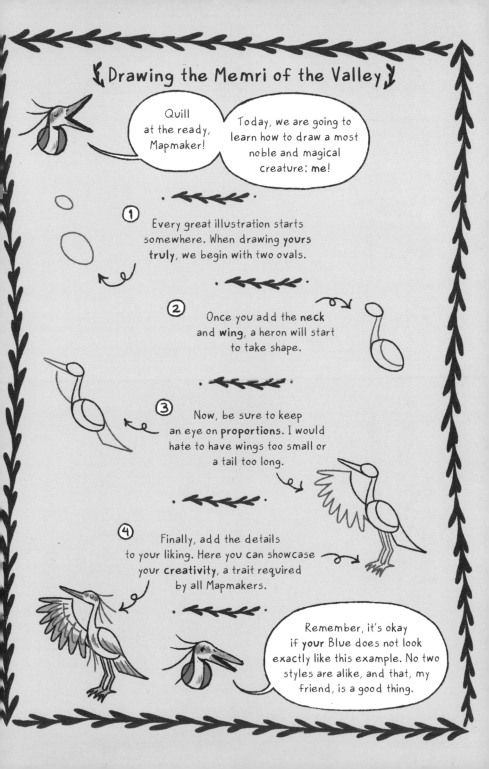

Ma's Tomato Jam

My mom taught me how to make this when I was a kid, but I've added a few wrinkles of my own over the years. Like all my favorite recipes, it's best when shared with others.

Ingredients:

- 6 medium-sized tomatoes, cored and chopped coarsely
- 1 small pepper of choice, minced
- 1/2 onion, minced
- 3-4 cloves of garlic, smashed then minced
- 1/2 tbsp of vegetable oil, for sautéing
- juice of 1 lemon
- 1/2 cup of brown sugar
- 1/2 tsp of paprika (smoked or regular)
- 1/2 tsp chili powder
- 1/4 tsp cinnamon
- 1 tsp coarse salt (use less if table salt)
- 1/2 tsp black pepper
- 1/4 tsp red pepper flakes (optional)
- drizzle of balsamic vinegar (optional)

Directions:

1. Heat up the vegetable oil over medium heat in a medium-sized pot. Once heated, sauté the onion and pepper in the oil until soft and fragrant. Add garlic and sauté until fragrant.

2. Add the tomatoes and stir well. Let it break down a little, until it reaches a gentle simmer.

3. Add the sugar, lemon juice, spices, and balsamic vinegar (if using). Mix well.

4. Reduce the heat to medium low or low and let the mixture simmer down until thickened. It should reduce to about half the amount it was from the start.

5. Once reduced, turn off the stove and let the mixture cool. Serve immediately, or put it in an airtight container and store for up to 2 weeks.

Making of a Page
From concept to final

PG85

PG86

PG87

maybe change
angle

PAGE 86

Panel 1: Vertical panel stretching the whole page as the two kids climb up the tree. Alidade's a little bit higher than Lewis, taking the fastest (and more adventurous) route. She's got her head up, constantly searching. Meanwhile, Lewis has got his eyes on the yellow-tailed ravens, perched in the tree and fluttering about.

ALIDADE: Keep your eye out for something special.

Panel 2: The first of three equal stacked panels to the right of the vertical panel. Lewis has stopped mid-reach for a branch when he spots the gnarly looking yellow-tailed perched there and eying him suspiciously.

LEWIS: Uh—these yellow-tailed ravens look more...**hungry** than special.

RAVEN: SQWAK!

Panel 3: On Alidade as she leaps off both feet from one sturdy branch to a bigger one higher up. She's really going for it.

ALIDADE: They're **birds**. They're not going to **eat** you.

Panel 4: View from level with this new higher branch as Alidade pulls herself up, a soft yellow-green light shining on her face.

ALIDADE: But I think I found what they **do** eat...

*see the final art on page 86!

Final Designs

Alternate Color Palettes

② ③ ④

Additional Character Designs

Younger Alidade and the Rose Family

The Briar Family

Constable Atwater and Night Coats Ada and Tace

When designing Alidade and Lewis, there were only a few key elements that Cam wanted to be included, such as Alidade's hat and scarf, as well as Lewis's glasses and short-cropped hair, but the rest was up to me. My intent with their designs was to have them play off of each other in a way that would make the other stand out even more, and for me, a good place to always start is understanding their personalities: Alidade, who is bold and always ready for adventure; Lewis, who is careful and a kindhearted, community-oriented kid.

In addition to Alidade and Lewis, I decided to create final designs for their respective families as well so that the two kids could feel more integrated into the world around them. Alidade's scarf is one of her distinctive features, so I gave her family their signature green tones to jump off of. Lewis comes from a big family with big personalities so I worked to figure out how to make each member individualized, as well as cohesive as a whole so that they really felt like they belonged together.

The Night Coats, on the other hand, served to create a contrast to the world where Alidade and Lewis come from. They're outsiders and not from the Valley, not really understanding the place and its true worth. The Night Coats' rigid and neutral-colored designs serve to separate them from the Valley folk, whose natural and humble designs tie them to the land.

Lodge Exterior Sketches

plants spilling out? No!

vine curtain

*magic glass allows you to see out & not be seen in.

balcony patio thing

Early Valley Lodge Designs

*DOUGLAS FIR!!

MAIN ROOM

EXTERIOR

FRONT

STAIRS

UPSTAIRS DOORS

LIBRARY

Valley Lodge Rough Layout

Designing the Valley Lodge was the most difficult task when it came to creating this world. There were certain points of inspiration that Cam provided: Frank Lloyd Wright's Cedar Rock, Wayfarers Chapel in California, and the idea that this lodge is integrated with its surroundings. Going off the idea that the doorway for this lodge is in a tree, I decided to keep that tree as the central point of the lodge. Since the lodge is a place for Mapmakers to travel through and take a rest, I also thought about what the coolest forest cabin would look like and what would be essential to travelers. To me, that's lots of high spaces, slanted ceilings, a big community kitchen area, and wide open windows to see all the greenery outside!

Note from the Writer

I have a terrible sense of direction. I get turned around easily, don't risk driving without a GPS, and lose my way on the most routine travels. This is true even when writing.

I can be deep into a script and realize I'm not sure how to get to the other side. Influences and inspirations change. What seemed like a perfect ending suddenly seems out of place.

In those moments during the writing of *Mapmakers and the Lost Magic*, I turned to the things that give me a feeling of home: My favorite places in Northeast Ohio, Southern California, and New England. The books and comics I devoured as a kid. Family and friends.

I knew that if I could somehow capture those feelings in Alidade's story, even just a tiny bit, I could guide her on this journey. After all, despite my frequent detours and wrong turns, I always find my way home.

Note from the Artist

When I read the first draft of this script, I thought it would tell a simple adventure story about a young girl who wanted to seek out and understand the secrets of the land she comes from. In a sense, it does, but while I worked on it, it became so much more to me.

The time I worked on this book has harbored some of the biggest changes in my life, and Alidade and her story have become an anchor point for me to hold on to. During the year and a half that I worked on this book, I came to the slow realization that Alidade reminds me of myself as a child, frustrated at the world and yearning to leave home to see what the world has in store, and encapsulates everything I wished I was when I was younger: brave, determined, and honest with herself.

Alidade's journey as a character has been such a special one for me because the lessons she learns and realizations she makes reminded me of those I had to come to understand when I was growing up and even to this day. Just like Alidade, I learned how important and powerful the community you come from or surround yourself with is, that there is so much that is better off done together, with the people you love and trust. And, along with Alidade, I have grown over the course of this book, further learning and understanding the traits that I had admired in her within myself.

Going into the design for Alidade, I knew that I wanted her to be a character I wished to see when I was a kid. Someone who's not defined by her appearance alone, but rather by the way she's able to act so unabashedly like herself. As Alidade and only Alidade. And now, as this book goes out into the hands of countless kids in the world, I hope she can inspire you the way she has inspired me. To me, Alidade's story is a representation that for every person who feels lost, there is a community —a beacon of light, a compass rose—ready to help guide you home.

Acknowledgments

While writing may be a solitary act, there are countless people in my corner who make it possible.

I can never give enough thanks to my entire family—the Chittocks, Njoyas, and Taylors—for their love and belief in me.

I would not even be a writer without the encouragement and patience of teachers like Michael Stahl, Lee Fallon, and Mildred Lewis.

During the development process, I received invaluable enthusiasm and feedback from Sierra Hahn, David Petersen, and Doug Smit. I was also lucky enough to join an incredible school community that supported me (and kept me sane) each and every day.

The wonderful folks at Random House Graphic believed in us from the beginning and worked tirelessly on behalf of this book. I need to specially thank our designer, Patrick Crotty, and our editor, Whitney Leopard. They deserve all the credit.

Comics is an artist's medium, and I'm so grateful to work with truly one of the best. Amanda's thoughtfulness, creativity, and collaboration made this story, and the experience of telling it, far better than I ever could have imagined.

Finally, no matter what stage of the writing process I was in, I got to end each day by sharing what I wrote with my best friend and favorite reader. Whatever I was working on, talking story with my wife, Tay, ensured I never felt like I was writing alone.

—Cameron

The journey of making a full graphic novel is never an easy one, especially the first time.

I'd like to thank our amazing editor, Whitney, and designer, Patrick, for all the patience, understanding, and words of encouragement they've given along the way. I really couldn't have asked for a greater team to help guide the telling and the look of this book in the right direction. I'd also like to extend this thanks to everyone at Random House Graphic and those involved with making this book what it was, for believing in this tale and everything we hoped to accomplish with it.

Going into this process for the first time was definitely intimidating, but working with a writer as thoughtful, creative, and supportive as Cam made it so much more possible to achieve what I thought I couldn't do. Every time he crafted new words or shared new ideas, I was only inspired more and more by this world. Thank you for believing in me and trusting me to assist with bringing your vision to life. To say I'm honored in helping it become a reality is a huge understatement.

My unending gratitude goes to Ryan Sands, for allowing me to assist with Youth in Decline as a wee baby college student who didn't know exactly what they wanted to do yet. Your unending love for comics and their creators inspired me, as well as helped me realize what it was I wanted to do and gave me the space to start creating stories I wanted to tell.

I'd like to thank my professors from college—Allan, Shadra, and Aya—for your belief in me as an artist. Without your support and motivation to challenge myself, I wouldn't be in the position I am today.

Finally, I'd like to thank all my loved ones. First and foremost, my mom and dad; my sister, Isabelle; as well as the rest of my family. You helped me grow up in an environment of love and encouragement, believing in me and what I do every single day. Without your endless support, I wouldn't be where I am right now and I couldn't express the gratitude and love I feel for you through words alone. To Sara, Victoria, Abelle, Angie, Emily (and Andy too!), Megan, Steph, Sara, Taylor, Sophie, and Emily: your friendship throughout the years has been and will always be irreplaceable. To be able to share this book with you isn't nearly enough thanks for all the support and love you've given me.

You are all my Alden. You are all my home.

The art for this book was created on the occupied lands of the Piscataway, Ohlone, and Onondaga (Seneca) peoples.

—Amanda

Cameron Chittock is a writer from Northeast Ohio. He grew up surrounded by siblings, wildlife, and comics of all kinds. Cameron's writing is possible thanks to patient teachers, encouraging friends, and a supportive family. His favorite stories are those of heroes and friendship. Cameron previously edited comics, including titles such as the Eisner Award–nominated graphic novel *New World*, *Mech Cadet Yu*, and *Jim Henson's The Power of the Dark Crystal*. He now lives in New England and works in education. When he's not writing, he enjoys coaching basketball, reading giant fantasy books, and sitting by the pond with his family. *Mapmakers and the Lost Magic* is his debut graphic novel.

cameronwtchittock.com
@CameronChittock

Amanda Castillo is a comic artist, illustrator, and storyteller, born and raised in the Bay Area in California. Having grown up inspired by piles of manga, games about friendship and adventure, and the endless wonders of the California outdoors, Amanda went on to study illustration to hone a skill set to tell warm and heartfelt stories that could be enjoyed and remembered by someone like you! After getting into the comics world through working with Youth in Decline, Amanda has since contributed to publishers such as BOOM! Studios, Lion Forge, and now Random House Graphic. In addition to making comics, Amanda has shown work in galleries domestically and helped judge annual comics awards. When not making comics, Amanda enjoys spending time with friends and loved ones, making warm and hearty meals, learning to tend to plants, and taking in the lovely moments the world has to offer. *Mapmakers and the Lost Magic* is their debut graphic novel.

amanda-castillo.com
@mandallin

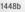